BIG
PROBLEMS
LITTLE
PROBLEMS

For Sam. Being your dad is my life's greatest joy.
—BF

To my father.
—ML

Text © 2022 by Ben Feller · Illustrations © 2022 by Mercè López

Hardcover ISBN 978-0-88448-890-3 · 10 9 8 7 6 5 4 3 2 1
Library of Congress Control Number: 2022931545

Tilbury House Publishers
Thomaston, Maine
www.tilburyhouse.com

Designed by Frame25 Productions
Printed in South Korea

BIG
PROBLEMS
LITTLE
PROBLEMS

Written by **Ben Feller**

Illustrated by
Mercè López

TILBURY HOUSE PUBLISHERS

Sam was getting ready for school.
Dad was getting ready for work.

Sam was trying to zip up his new coat but could not figure out how to do it.

DAD!
I have a BIG problem!

Dad walked over to Sam and showed him how to
line up the grooves and pull the zipper up tight.

ZIP!

"There you go," said Dad.
"Now was that a big problem, or a little problem?"

Sam wasn't sure what the difference was.
He just knew he felt a lot better.

"Well, not being able to zip your coat
might feel like a big problem," said Dad.

"But in perspective, it's really
just a little problem."

"Per . . . what?" asked Sam.

"Perspective," said Dad.
"It's how you look at things."

Sam and Dad gave each other a

big hug,

did their secret handshake,

SLAP!

SNAP!

TAP!

and off they went.

The next morning, Sam
had another problem.

He could not find his superhero cape
he wanted to wear to school that day.

Sam and his dad looked all around,
but they could not find the cape.

They searched Sam's closet, under his bed,

and even in the bathroom . . .

NO CAPE.

Dad suggested that Sam take his favorite stuffed animal instead. It wasn't exactly what Sam wanted, but he agreed it was fine.

"Now," said Dad, "was that a big problem or a little problem?"

"A little problem," Sam said.

"Good," said Dad. "I just don't want you to get frustrated."

"Frus . . . what?" asked Sam.

"Frustrated," said Dad. "It's that feeling you get when you can't figure things out."

"Do you ever feel that way?" asked Sam.
"Absolutely," said Dad. "Grown-ups get frustrated too."

"When I get frustrated," Dad continued, "I take three deep breaths, and then I feel better. Want to try it with me?"

Sam and Dad closed their eyes . . .

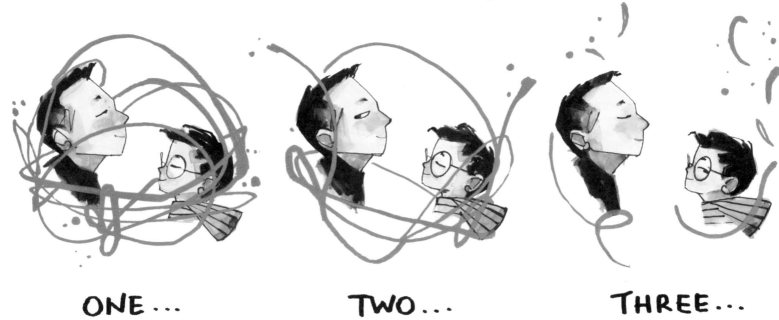

ONE . . .   TWO . . .   THREE . . .

Then they gave each other a big hug,

The next morning, Sam ran into
the kitchen to tell Dad that

he had found his superhero cape!

But before he could even say where he'd found it,
Sam accidentally bumped into Dad's coffee . . .

spilling it all over the table, onto Dad's
important papers, and onto the floor.

"Don't get frustrated, Dad," said Sam. "Can you call your boss and tell her you are going to be late?"

"Yes, I can do that," said Dad.

"And can you make another cup of coffee?" asked Sam.

"Well, sure I can do that," said Dad.

"And can you get another set of papers?" asked Sam.

"Yes, I can do that, too," said Dad.

"So, are these *big problems* or *little problems*?" asked Sam.

"Little problems," said Dad.

"I just want you to have . . . perspective," said Sam.

Dad smiled. "You certainly are teaching me to have more patience," he said.

"Pay . . . what?" said Sam.

"Patience," said Dad.

"It means staying calm even if things feel busy."

Sam and Dad cleaned up the spill together.

Dad called his boss and made another cup of coffee. Dad reprinted his paperwork.

Sam wore his superhero cape over his new coat.

ZIP!

They were just about to walk
out the door when Sam said . . .

DAD!

We have a
BIG
PROBLEM!

"We do?" said Dad.
"We forgot something," said Sam.

Dad checked his pockets, his work bag, and Sam's
backpack. He could not figure out what was missing.

"What did we forget, Sam?" asked Dad.

"We forgot our hug!" Sam said.
Then Dad got down on his knees and gave Sam a big hug.

They did their secret handshake,

And just to be sure, they took three deep breaths. ONE... TWO... THREE...

"Thank you," said Dad.
"No problem," said Sam.

And off they went.

Ben Feller is a communications advisor and a former award-winning chief White House correspondent for The Associated Press. During his years of covering Presidents Barack Obama and George W. Bush, he was a leader of the White House press corps, traveled aboard Air Force One around the world, and was honored as a "master of deadline reporting." Now he is writing about his personal passion: being a dad. This is his first book.

Mercè López graduated from Llotja Art School in Barcelona, Spain, and has illustrated for design, theater, and film as well as forty children's books. Her illustrations for *I Am Smoke* (Tilbury House, 2021) were called "lustrous" and "exquisitely beautiful" in a starred review by *Kirkus*.